Bear and Hare
Snow!

Emily Gravett

MACMILLAN CHILDREN'S BOOKS

One morning, Bear and Hare
went outside and saw . . .

OW!

Hare loves snow.

Bear and Hare caught snowflakes
on their tongues.

They made snow prints,

and snow angels.

Bear rolled a big snowball,

and Hare rolled a little snowball.

LOTS of little snowballs!

SLEDGING!

Hare and Bear LOVE snow!

First
published 2014 by Macmillan Children's Books

an imprint of Pan Macmillan
20 New Wharf Road, London
N1 9RR

Associated companies throughout
the world
www.panmacmillan.com
ISBN: 978-1-5098-2929-3

For Fin

1 3 5 7 9 8 6 4 2

A CIP catalogue record
for this book is
available from
the British
Library.
Printed
in
China

The
Odd
Egg

Emily Gravett

ISBN: 978-0-230-53135-2

Orange
Pear
Apple
Bear

Emily Gravett

ISBN: 978-1-4050-9022-3

All Pan Macmillan titles
can be ordered from our website,
www.panmacmillan.com,
or from your local bookshop.

Monkey and ME

Emily Gravett

KATE
GREENAWAY
MEDAL

ISBN: 978-0-230-01583-8

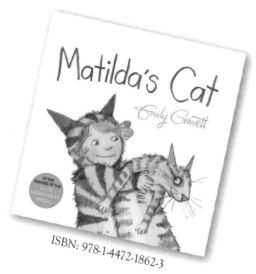

Matilda's Cat

Emily Gravett

KATE
GREENAWAY
MEDAL

ISBN: 978-1-4472-1862-3

KATE
GREENAWAY
MEDAL

Emily Gravett

DOGS

ISBN: 978-0-230-71248-5

www.emilygravett.com